IMOGENE'S

IMOGENE'S ANTLERS

By David Small

SCHOLASTIC INC.
NEW YORK TORONTO LONDON AUCKLAND SYDNEY

ISBN 0-590-42026-7

 Published by Scholastic Inc., 730 Broadway, New York, NY 10003, by arrangement with Crown Publishers, Inc.

12 11 10 9 2 3/9

Printed in the U.S.A. 09

First Scholastic printing, October 1988

To A.B., L.D. and little O.

—D.S.

On Thursday, when Imogene
woke up, she found she
had grown antlers.

Getting dressed was difficult,

and going through a door
now took some thinking.

Imogene started down
for breakfast…

but got
hung up.

"OH!!"
Imogene's mother
fainted away.

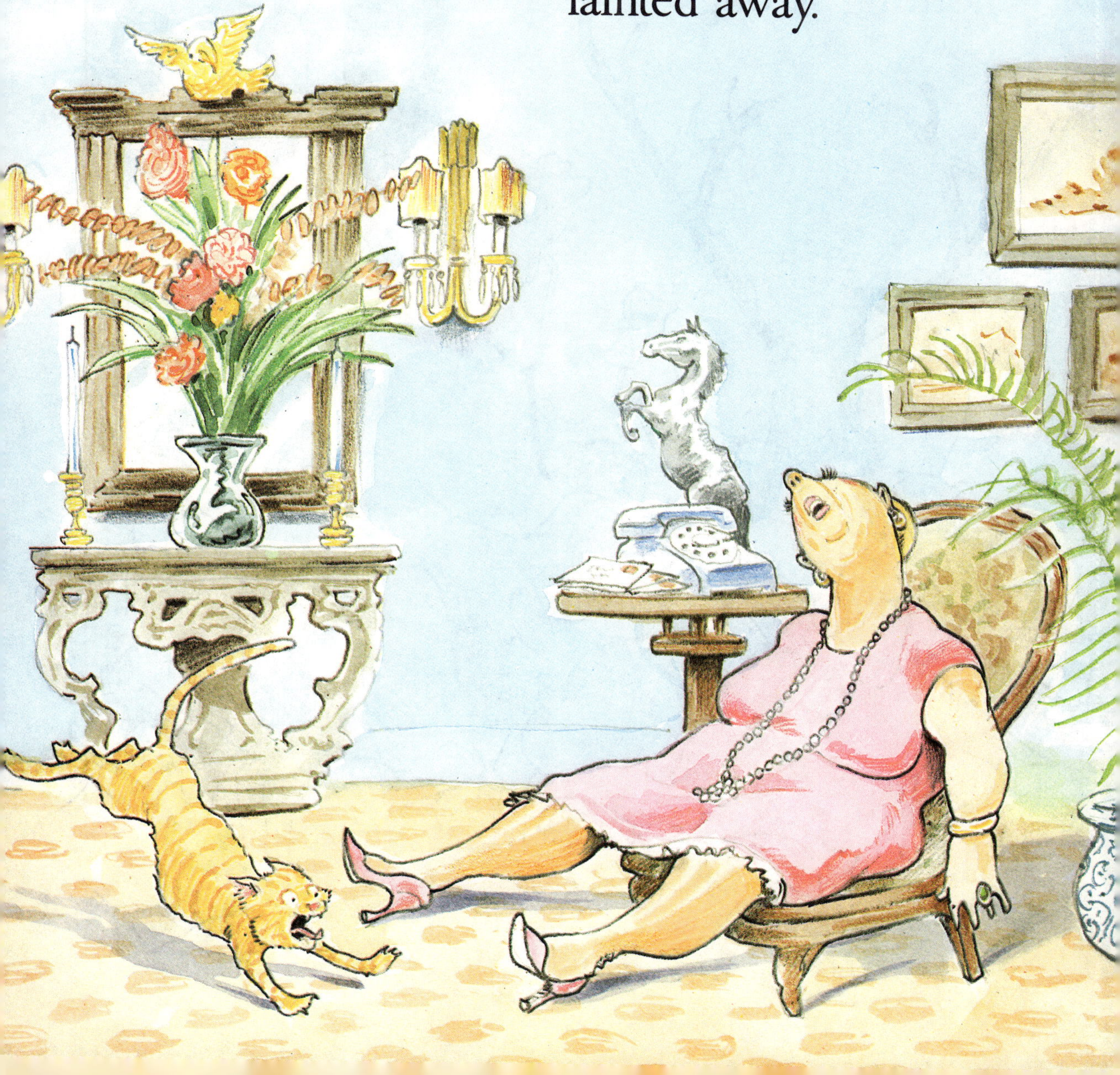

The doctor poked, and prodded, and scratched his chin.

He could find nothing wrong.

The school principal glared at Imogene but had no advice to offer.

Her brother, Norman, consulted the encyclopedia, and then announced that Imogene had turned into a rare form of miniature elk!

Imogene's mother fainted again
and was carried upstairs to bed.

Imogene went into the kitchen. Lucy, the kitchen maid, had her sit by the oven to dry some towels.

"Lovely antlers," said Lucy.

The cook, Mrs. Perkins, gave
Imogene a doughnut, then
decked her out with several more
and sent her into the garden
to feed the birds.

"You'll be lots of fun
to decorate,
come Christmas!"
said Mrs. Perkins.

Later, Imogene wandered upstairs.
She found the whole family
in Mother's bedroom.

"Doughnuts anyone?" she asked.

Her mother said, “Imogene, we have decided there is only one thing to do. We must hide your antlers under a hat!”

Norman telephoned the milliner.

At three o'clock
the milliner
arrived.

Rapidly
he sketched
a few designs,

then set to work.

"Voilà!"
said the
milliner.

*"Bravo!
Bravissimo!"*
cried his
assistants.

THUD!
Imogene's mother
had to be carried away
once more.

After dinner,
Imogene practiced
her piano
lesson.

Then, yawning,
she folded her music...

kissed the family...

and went to bed.

Imogene sighed,
remembering the long,
eventful day.

On Friday, when Imogene
woke up, the antlers had disappeared.

When she came down to breakfast, the family was overjoyed to see her back to normal...

until she came into the room.